Resurrection Day

by

Alice Huffaker

Illustrated by Keith Neely

MOODY PRESS

CHICAGO

For all my young teachers

©1990 by
ALICE L. HUFFAKER

ISBN: 0-8024-2638-7

Moody Press, a ministry of the Moody Bible Institute,
is designed for education, evangelization, and edification.
If we may assist you in knowing more about Christ
and the Christian life, please write us without obligation:
Moody Press, c/o MLM, Chicago, Illinois 60610.

1 2 3 4 5 6 Printing/DP/Year 94 93 92 91 90

Printed in the United States of America

Soldiers, soldiers,

what would you say

if you could tell us all about

resurrection day?

Children, children,

we would say,

"An angel rolled the stone away

on resurrection day."

Angels, angels,

what would you say

if you could tell us all about

resurrection day?

Children, children,

we would say,

"Christ Jesus came to life again

on resurrection day."

Women, women,

what would you say

if you could tell us all about

resurrection day?

Children, children,

we would say,

"We ran to tell the happy news

on resurrection day."

Friend John, friend John,

what would you say

if you could tell us all about

resurrection day?

Children, children,

I would say

"We quickly ran to Jesus' grave

on resurrection day."

Peter, Peter,

what would you say

if you could tell us all about

resurrection day?

Children, children,

I would say,

"The risen Jesus talked to me

on resurrection day."

Mary, Mary,

what would you say

if you could tell us all about

resurrection day?

Children, children,

I would say,

"Christ Jesus is alive because

of resurrection day."

Good friends, good friends,

what would you say

if you could tell us all about

resurrection day?

Children, children,

we would say,

"The body of the Lord was gone

on resurrection day."

Children, children,

what will YOU say

when you are asked to tell about

resurrection day?